MY TEACHER DAD

Written by Sonya Annita Song
Illustrated by Kate Fallahee

Chinchilla Books

ISBN 978-1-9995402-6-5 (hardback)
ISBN 978-1-9995402-7-2 (paperback)
ISBN 978-1-9995402-8-9 (ebook)

Published by Chinchilla Books
Printed in Korea
chinchillabooks@gmail.com
www.chinchillabooks.ca

For all the boys and girls

With teacher dads and teacher moms.

"I don't want to go to school today. Pooh," my teacher whined.

"Oh, not again," I told my dad.
"I know you're feeling fine."

"Oh no, I'm not! My tummy hurts!"
Said teacher who's my dad

While curling up into a ball
And making his face sad.

"Well, Dad, I'm going to count to ten,
And then I'm telling Mom."

My dad then jolted out of bed
As if I'd dropped a bomb.

WHACK!

Then finally, we got to school,
But teacher had not come.

I found him in the teachers' lounge
With skates and chewing gum.

He jumped and said,
"Then let's play tag!
And tag, YOU'RE IT!"
While spinning as he fled.

"Squad One. You're up. It won't be fun. It's Monday Protocol."

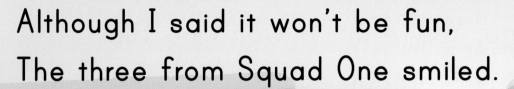
Although I said it won't be fun,
The three from Squad One smiled.

They grabbed their skates.
I taught the class, although I was a child.

"Then please be good!" was my reply,
Arriving at the house.

"I have a cold," my father sniffed.
"I think I'm going to choke!"

"GET UP!" I roared. "I know you're fine!"
I gave him my best glare.

"I know you want to read all day.
I see your comics there!"

"Boo-hoo! You're mean!" my father cried
While grumping to his feet

And humphed into his teaching suit
While I went down to eat.

At least to school we were on time.
He even came to class.

But then at lunch he disappeared -
I found him in the grass.

BOUNCE!

Well, rolling in the grass, that is,
And boy, that man could roll!

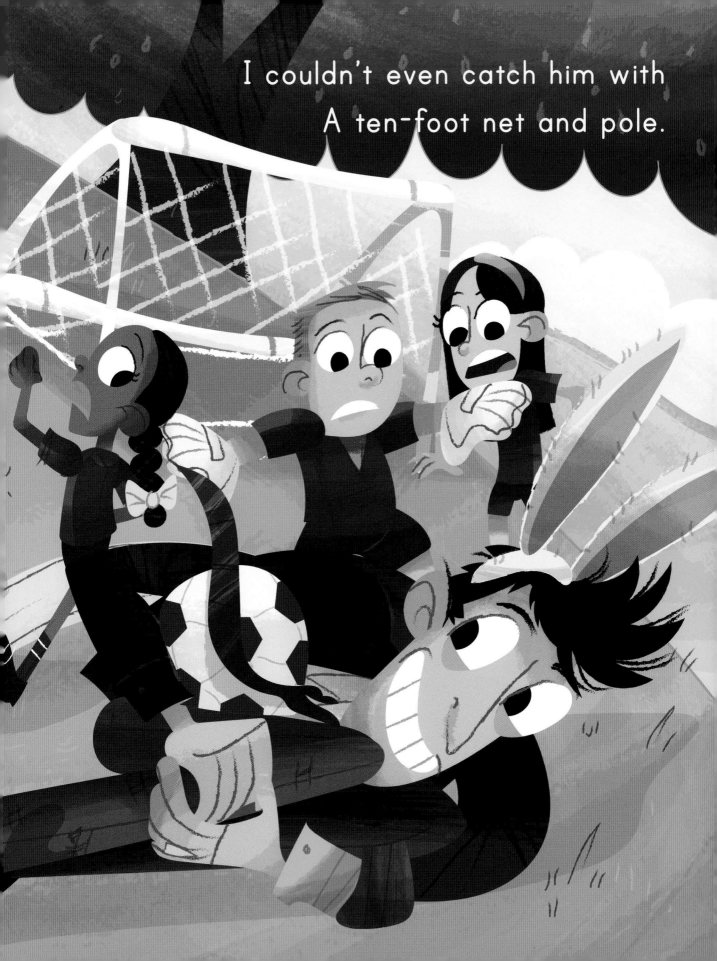

I couldn't even catch him with
A ten-foot net and pole.